Fashion Fairy Princess

Thanks and Sparkles, Catherine Coe!

First published in the UK in 2014 by Scholastic Children's Books
An imprint of Scholastic Ltd
Euston House, 24 Eversholt Street
London, NW1 1DB, UK
Registered office: Westfield Road, Southam, Warwickshire, CV47 0RA
SCHOLASTIC and associated logos are trademarks and/or registered
trademarks of Scholastic Inc.

Text copyright © Scholastic Ltd, 2014
Cover copyright © Pixie Potts, Beehive Illustration Agency, 2014
Inside illustration copyright © David Shephard, The Bright Agency, 2014

The right of Poppy Collins to be identified as the author
of this work has been asserted by her.

ISBN 978 1407 14751 2

A CIP catalogue record for this book is available from the British Library

Printed and bound by CPI Group (UK) Ltd, Croydon, CR0 4YY

Papers used by Scholastic Children's Books are made
from wood grown in sustainable forests.

1 3 5 7 9 10 8 6 4 2

This is a work of fiction. Names, characters, places,
incidents and dialogues are products of the author's imagination
or are used fictitiously. Any resemblance to actual people, living
or dead, events or locales is entirely coincidental.

www.scholastic.co.uk
www.fashionfairyprincess.com

Fashion Fairy Princess

Holly

🍃 and the Christmas Wish 🍃

POPPY COLLINS

■SCHOLASTIC

Dream
Mountain

Jewel Forest

Sparkle
City

Star
Valley

River
Sapphire

Shimmer Island

Glitter Ocean

Welcome to the world of the fashion fairy princesses! Join Holly and friends on their magical adventures in fairyland.

They can't wait to explore

Sparkle City!

Can you?

Chapter 1

Holly pressed her
nose against the
circular window
of her pink brick
cottage. Outside,
Sparkle City
looked just like
a Christmas card. It had been snowing for
over a week, and everything was covered
in a glittery snow carpet. The trees, plants,

houses and shops were so white and sparkly that the landscape seemed even more magical than usual.

Instead of shopping or running errands, all the fairies in the city seemed to be playing in the snow. Holly watched two fairies fly past, pulling sledges behind them. At the corner of her street, a group were making a fairy snowman, and in the distance she could see fairies laughing and having a snowball fight.

A knock on the door made Holly jump. She fluttered over, pulled it open, and smiled to see the flushed faces of her best friends, May and Summer.

Summer held up her skis. "We're going to play on Harmony Hill – are you coming?"

Holly grinned. "Yes, please!"

"I'm going to try and beat my
downhill record!" said May. Holly could
barely see her brown eyes underneath the
lilac woolly hat she was wearing.

"Come inside while I get my things,"
said Holly.

May and Summer flew in and nestled
into Holly's peacock-feather sofa, while

Holly pulled on a turquoise hat over her shoulder-length blonde hair, then slipped on matching gloves and coat. Finally, she grabbed her skis and boots from the cupboard.

"OK, I'm ready!" Holly declared.

As soon as she got outside, Holly was glad she'd wrapped up warmly – the air was chilly, and it was still snowing. The fairies could see their breath as they spoke.

"I can't believe it's nearly Christmas!" said Summer, her long auburn hair peeking out from under a velvet hat. "I wonder if we'll get invited to the Snowflake Ball this year?"

"Oh, I'd so *love* to go," May said. "It's meant to be the most magical party in all of fairyland!"

The Snowflake Ball was held every

year, on Christmas Eve, in the enchanted grounds of Glimmershine Palace. The palace was a beautiful sparkly building with lots of gorgeous turrets and stained-glass windows. It was where all the fairy royalty lived – including the fairy princesses. Every fairy in fairyland, let alone Sparkle City, was desperate for an invitation to the ball. But not everyone could go – only a handful of fairies were invited each year.

"I wonder how the fairy princesses decide?" said Holly. "I don't think I've done anything special enough to deserve an invite."

"At least your name *sounds* Christmassy," said Summer with a wink. "May and I don't really sound like we'd fit in at a winter ball!"

Holly laughed. She hadn't thought of

that – although she was pretty sure that wasn't how the fairy princesses chose their guests.

The three fairies carried their skis right to the top of Harmony Hill. Within seconds, May had strapped hers on and whizzed away down the steepest slope. Holly grinned at her fearless friend, whose golden wings had become a blur. There was no way she'd be going that fast! Luckily, Summer also preferred the gentler slope, and the two fairies were soon skiing down it together. They waved at May as she passed them, already flying back up the hill.

"I'm much too clumsy to go as fast as May," said Summer as she and Holly glided to a stop at the bottom. "I'd end up toppling over and getting my head stuck in the snow!"

Holly nodded in agreement. She loved zooming down the hill, fluttering her light-blue wings in the wind, but she was only a little fairy and she liked to enjoy skiing at a steady pace.

After they'd been up and down several times, they bumped into May at the bottom of the hill. "Shall we do snow fairies now?" suggested Summer.

"What are snow fairies?" asked May.

Holly smiled. "You don't know? Let me show you!" The petite fairy jumped on to her back in the soft, newly fallen snow and fluttered her wings to make a fairy shape.

Summer laid down next to her and did the same thing with her own cherry-red wings.

"Oh, that looks like so much fun!" said May, jumping down on the other side of Holly. The friends squealed as they felt the cold snow through their warm clothes.

"How about we go and get some hot chocolate to

warm up?" suggested Holly. It was her favourite drink, especially in wintertime.

"Good idea!" said Summer. All three fairies fluttered up and brushed the glittering snow off their clothes.

They were soon sitting in Cutey-Pie Café sipping hot chocolate topped with pink whipped cream. The hot drink tasted sweet, smooth and creamy in Holly's mouth, warming her up from her toes to the tips of her wings.

May looked through the café windows, which were edged with rainbow fairy lights. "It's getting dark," she said.

Holly nodded as she turned to look at the dusky sky. The snow was still falling heavily from the fluffy clouds. "We should probably go home. But we can play in the snow again tomorrow, can't we?"

"Oh, yes!" said Summer. "It looks like

there'll be lots more snow too!"

May and Summer lived a few streets away from Holly, so she said goodbye at the corner of her road, holding her skis in one hand and waving with the other. "See you tomorrow!"

Holly turned into her street, and grinned as she thought about what a fun day it had been. But her smile turned to a frown when she noticed something strange outside her cottage – a white carriage with a royal crest, and some fairy-bunnies jumping out of the back. She hoped she wasn't in trouble. Whatever could it be about?

Chapter 2

Holly fluttered along slowly, worrying about the carriage outside her cottage. Perhaps she had forgotten to pay this month's fairy bills? She shook her head. No – she was sure she'd posted the fairy-dust in time.

As she got closer, she noticed that one of the fairy-bunnies held a little golden trumpet in his paws. Now Holly was really confused. The fairy-bunny brought the instrument up to his mouth, took a deep breath and began to play a trumpet fanfare.

Is this really for me? Holly wondered. By now she'd reached the pavement outside her cottage where the carriage stood. The fairy-bunny ended the fanfare as a second bunny flew up to Holly, cradling something in his paws. Holly felt her hands shaking as the fairy-bunny passed it to her gently – it was a sparkling letter in the shape of a snowflake!

The little fairy let out a gasp as she read the blue-glitter handwriting:

Dear Holly,

   We are delighted to invite you to this year's Snowflake Ball at Glimmershine Palace.

   You will be collected at 6 p.m., on Christmas Eve, by a carriage pulled by winged ponies.

*Please dress in your most magical party
outfit!*

With lots of love and fairy wishes,

Princesses Rosa, Bluebell, Violet and

Buttercup xxx

Holly couldn't believe her eyes. An
invitation to the Snowflake Ball! As she
stared at it in shock, it melted away
into nothing. She turned to the fairy-
bunnies.

"Is it true? Am I invited? Why did the
invitation disappear?"

The bunny with the trumpet smiled.
"The ball is so special that only the
fairies who are invited are allowed to
know the details," he squeaked. "Can you
remember them?"

Holly nodded, her heart racing with

excitement. "Six o'clock, on Christmas Eve!"

"That's right," said the bunny who'd given Holly the invitation. "See you then!"

As the fairy bunnies bowed and hopped back into the royal carriage, Holly suddenly realized what that meant. She had only two days to get ready for the ball!

She watched as the grand white carriage sped off into the distance and disappeared through the snow. She wondered whether they were delivering more invitations, and who else would get one. She hoped from the bottom of her heart that Summer and May would be invited too.

Holly fluttered towards her cottage, smiling at the roof that was now white with snow rather than its usual pink. Icicles dangled down prettily from the roof. She knew lots of fairies loved the warmth and sunshine of the summer, but winter was definitely Holly's favourite time of year – and now she was going to the ball!

Once inside, Holly threw some fairy-dust on the fire, and the logs began to burn brightly, lighting up the room. She took off her coat, hat, gloves and boots and sat down on the sofa. But she was so excited that she started bouncing up and down – she couldn't sit still! Then she remembered that the invitation had said to wear her most magical party outfit. She jumped up and fluttered to her oak wardrobe, flinging open the doors and staring at the clothes inside.

Holly pulled out dress after dress, skirt after skirt, blouse after blouse, but she soon realized that she had nothing suitable for such a special ball. She'd have to go shopping. She'd need to get new shoes too. And what about her hair?

All Holly thought about that evening was the Snowflake Ball. She ate a dinner of toadstool-topped toast, followed by a red velvet cupcake, and wondered what delicious food and drinks might be served

at the ball. When she snuggled down
into her cotton-fur bed, she found sleep
just wouldn't come. She couldn't stop
thinking about all the things she needed
to do, and where she was going to find
the perfect dress. Holly tossed and turned,
wondering what the ball would be like,
who would be there, and if she'd fit in

among the other special guests. And when she finally managed to get to sleep, she dreamt strange dreams of riding in a winged carriage that took her to a party so covered in snow that she couldn't see anything but white. . .

Chapter 3

Holly woke with a start, jumped out of bed and flew over to the window. Outside, the glistening snowflakes were falling just as heavily as yesterday. With no time to waste, Holly quickly poured herself a bowl of fairy-fruit muesli, and planned her day while she munched.

First she'd go to see Summer and May – she was desperate to find out if they'd been invited to the ball as well.

Then she would go shopping for the perfect ball gown – with shoes to match, of course. She hoped that all the shops in Sparkle City Mall would still be open this close to Christmas!

Holly cleaned her teeth with her diamond-topped toothbrush then pulled on her coat and boots. She glanced out of the window – it was still snowing. She'd definitely need her hat and gloves today.

She made sure she had lots of fairy-dust in her blue leather satchel, then pushed open her front door. The snow had piled up so much overnight that she had to shove the door with her shoulder to get it to budge!

Minutes later, Holly knocked on the door of Summer's house. It too was covered in snow, the white glittery grains

hiding the pretty yellow bricks. The door
opened almost immediately.

"Oh, hi, Holly!" said Summer. "Why
are you up so early?"

Oh dear, thought Holly. *It doesn't sound as
if Summer has been invited to the ball after all!*
Surely she would have mentioned it right
away. Now Holly didn't know what to say.

"I . . . erm. . . You see. . ."

Summer frowned. "What's the matter? Is everything OK?"

Holly bit her lip. "Oh, yes, I'm fine — it's just that I've . . . been invited to the Snowflake Ball. . ." She said this last bit so quietly that Summer could barely hear her.

"That's fantastic!" Summer jumped up and down. "Why didn't you say so?"

"Because I was hoping that you'd been invited too," Holly said, looking down. "I wanted us to go dress shopping together. Now I feel bad."

Summer gave her friend a hug. "Don't be silly! I never thought I'd be invited — but

I'm so excited for you. We must go dress shopping, of course!"

Summer's such a good friend, thought Holly. *She doesn't seem to mind at all.*

The two friends were soon ringing the doorbell of May's house in the next street along.

May came to the door in her star-print pyjamas, rubbing the sleep from her eyes.

"Hello, you two. You're early — I've only just woken up!"

"Holly's got some exciting news, haven't you?" Summer nudged Holly.

"Well, yes. . . I've been invited to the Snowflake Ball!"

May squealed so loudly Holly had to cover her ears. "That's the best news ever!"

Holly gave her a small smile. "But I was hoping you and Summer would have been invited as well. . ."

* *₊* 23 *₊* *

May shook her head, making her dark curly ringlets bounce around. "I haven't, I'm afraid – but it's amazing that one of us gets to go. Are we going shopping?"

"How did you guess?" said Summer with a wink. The fairy friends loved shopping together.

May zoomed off to get changed and was back within minutes wearing a huge red padded jacket. "It looks freezing out there!" she explained, pointing at the thick snow falling from the white fluffy clouds. "I want to keep warm!"

As they flew towards Diamond Boulevard Holly felt a warm feeling bubble up inside. OK, so her friends weren't coming to the ball with her, but at least they'd have a day of fun getting ready. *I'm so lucky to have friends like these*, Holly thought to herself.

Holly pushed open the door of Sparkle Sensations – their favourite clothes shop in the city – and the three fairies fluttered inside.

"Hello, girls!" called out the owner, Topaz. "You're my first customers today! What can I help you with?"

"We need a dress for the Snowflake Ball!" said Summer.

Topaz beamed. "Oh, how wonderful – are you all going?"

May shook her head, but smiled. "No, just Holly – but Summer and I are helping her to get ready. It's almost as good as going to the ball, anyway!"

Holly looked around with a bewildered expression, not knowing where to start with all the hundreds of dresses, skirts, tops and trousers that filled the shop. The clothes were organized by colour, so it felt a bit like being inside a rainbow! "Um . . . I'd like a dress – a ball gown, I

think. But I have no idea what might suit
me. . ."

Topaz fluttered over and put an arm
around Holly. "Don't worry — that's what
I'm here for. You girls sit down while I
choose some dresses for you to try on."

The three friends watched as Topaz
zoomed around the shop at top speed, piling
up more and more dresses in her arms.

"OK, try these!" Topaz said, her blue
eyes twinkling. She liked nothing more
than picking the perfect outfit for a fairy.

Holly fluttered behind the velvet
dressing-room curtain. Moments later, she
came out in a blue taffeta ball gown.

"Oh, it's lovely," said Summer.

"And it goes really well with your
hair," May added.

Holly flew in front of the floor-to-
ceiling mirror. She agreed it was a nice

dress, but it didn't seem quite *magical* enough. And it was far too long – she didn't want to trip over at the ball! She flew back into the dressing room to try on the next one.

This time she emerged wearing an emerald-green gown, with long lace sleeves and a neckline dotted with jewels. "I like this one too," Holly said, "but I might get too hot when I'm dancing."

May, Summer and Topaz all nodded.
"Yes, you're right."

Luckily, there were many more dresses
to try on. Holly changed into a pink
cotton dress with a netted skirt, then a
turquoise tutu skirt with a fitted jacket.
There was a shiny black silk dress with
a long train, and a lilac satin ball gown
with matching satin gloves.

But it wasn't until the very last dress
that she got the reaction she'd been
hoping for.

"Oh, wow!" May and Summer
murmured together, their mouths gaping
open.

"Now that *is* magical!" said Topaz.

Holly's heart raced as she spun around
in the shimmering white ball gown.
The embroidered snowflakes caught the
light as she turned. It fitted perfectly, the

sparkly hem just skimming the floor.

"This is the one!" said Holly, unable to take her eyes off the beautiful dress in the mirror.

Topaz grinned. "It's perfect for the ball. And did you know the snowflakes on it are real? They're specially made with fairy magic to make sure they don't melt!"

Holly felt so special wearing the dress that she didn't want to take it

off, but there was still lots to do and it was already lunchtime. She changed back into her clothes and put on her coat and gloves, then paid Topaz for the ball gown with two handfuls of fairy-dust.

Holly carried the dress carefully in its bag as she left the shop. That was one thing done for the ball. Next, she had to find the perfect shoes to match!

Chapter 4

"Oh, I love shoes *so* much," said Summer as the friends fluttered into Shining Shoes after a delicious lunch of purple-pepper soup at the Cutey-Pie Café. "I just wish my feet weren't so big!" She stared down at the large boots on her feet and pulled a face.

Holly grinned. "It's because you're so tall. But my feet are tiny — it's hard to find shoes small enough to fit!"

However, it didn't take long for Holly
to find the right shoes for her dress.
In the window display stood the most
elegant shoes she'd ever seen: white satin
pumps, with a stunning diamond sparkling
at the toe.

"Do you have them in my size?" she asked the shop owner, a fairy with dark cropped hair called Pearl.

"I think you're in luck," said Pearl. "These shoes have just arrived today. We've got them in every fairy size – but I think they'll sell out quickly!"

Holly slipped on the shoes. They were so soft inside it felt like she could dance in them for hours. The diamonds sparkled when she moved – they'd match the snowflakes on her dress perfectly.

The blonde fairy couldn't stop smiling as she paid for the gorgeous shoes. Then the three friends fluttered out of the shop and spent the rest of the afternoon helping Holly find accessories for her outfit. She bought a stunning white faux-fur wrap to keep her warm while she travelled to the ball, and the prettiest snowdrop hairclips to pin in her hair.

That night, Holly knew she'd have no trouble getting to sleep after such a busy day. She looked through her window at the snow that still fell, glistening in the air. Tomorrow was the day of the ball – she couldn't wait!

The next morning, Holly woke up feeling both excited and nervous. She had to pinch herself when she thought about going to the ball that evening – she still couldn't quite believe it was true! As she got ready to go to the hairdresser's, Holly realized she'd need to take her butterfly umbrella with her — the snow was falling so thickly she could barely see through her window.

She met Summer and May at Hair by Fairy, inside Sparkle City Mall. The three fairies loved this hairdresser's, not only because Sophia, the fairy who ran it, did the most amazing hairstyles, but also because the whole salon was decorated with tiny firefly lights. These reflected in the mirrors along both walls, so that they seemed to go on for ever.

"What are you going to have done to your hair?" asked May as Holly waited to be shown to a styling chair.

Holly looked at her friend. In all the excitement she hadn't given this any thought and really had no idea! But seeing May's natural ringlets, she suddenly knew what she wanted.

"Lots of curls all over, please!" she said
to Sophia. "And then I'd like it pinned
up with these snowdrop hairclips. If that
sounds OK?"

"Oh yes," said Sophia. "That's a great
choice for the Snowflake Ball!"

Summer and May chatted away while
Sophia worked on Holly's blonde hair.
When she'd finished, she held up a mirror
to show Holly the back and sides. Holly
gasped, finding it difficult to believe she was

looking at her own hair. It looked so pretty.

"Wow, Sophia! Thank you – it's beautiful!"

As the fairies left, Holly spotted Princess Violet sitting down to have her own hair done. Violet had long dark curly hair – the opposite of Holly's – and her fairy hairdresser began twisting it into a pretty bun on top of her head. Holly wondered what the other fairy princesses would do with their hair – but she knew they'd all look gorgeous!

The three friends fluttered along to the shop next door – Beauty Belle.

"I think I'll get my nails done too," said May.

"Oh yes, me three!" agreed Summer. "Having a manicure is so much more fun if you do it together!"

The fairies sat next to each other as the fairy manicurists clipped, filed and buffed their nails. Then they selected their nail polish colours.

Holly chose a sparkling silver colour to match her dress. Summer picked out a Christmassy berry red, and May decided on a shimmery green. "It'll make me look like a mermaid!" she told her friends.

The day passed very quickly, and soon Holly had to leave her friends in the mall to go home and change. She wanted to be ready in plenty of time for the carriage to pick her up at six o'clock.

Holly huddled under her umbrella

as she fluttered home. The wind blew
sparkly snow all around her, and she
didn't want to ruin her hair. She had to
fly because the snow on the ground came
up to her waist! There were only a few
fairies on the streets of Sparkle City now,
and those Holly did see were rushing
home under umbrellas or wearing woolly
hats. They fluttered above the thick snow
until they reached their cosy cottages and
hid away from the cold.

Back at home, Holly added fairy-
dust to her fire to keep warm as she
got ready, then carefully stepped into the
shimmering ball gown. It was incredible
to think that even in front of the heat of
her fire, the snowflakes on the dress didn't
melt. Holly was so excited that her hands
shook as she fastened up the zip.

But once she'd finished getting ready

and looked out of her window, Holly's excitement turned to worry. The snow whirling around outside looked more like a blizzard now, and it was terribly foggy too. She knew the winged ponies were magical, but could they fly through such bad weather to reach her?

Chapter 5

The blizzard seemed to be getting heavier and heavier. Holly kept glancing between the golden heart-shaped clock on her mantelpiece and the window. It was just five minutes to six. She stared and stared through the glass, hoping to make out the royal carriage in the distance, but all she could see was snow.

Bing, bing, bing, bing, bing, bing! The sound of her clock chiming made Holly jump at first — then she looked at it sadly. It was six o'clock. The ponies and carriage weren't here. *Maybe the snow's made them a little late*, she told herself, trying to stay cheery. They'd probably have to fly quite slowly in this weather.

Then something else made Holly jump. A tiny tapping sound was coming from the window! She fluttered over and saw a little robin shivering on the window sill. The poor thing! She opened the window quickly and the bird flew inside. Cold air blasted through the gap as she did, making Holly shiver too. She pushed the window closed as the robin perched on her clock on the mantlepiece, looking much happier to be near the warm fire.

It held a letter in its beak and, as Holly held out a hand, it dropped it on to her palm. She ripped open the wet red envelope. The paper inside was damp, but she could still read the writing:

Dear Snowflake Ball guest,

We are sorry to inform you that due to the blizzard, the winged ponies and royal butterflies are unable to collect any more guests for the ball. Please could we ask you to make your own way to Glimmershine Palace?

Stay safe, and we look forward to seeing you soon!

From Princesses Rosa, Bluebell, Violet and Buttercup xxx

Holly looked from the letter up to the window. *How in fairyland will I get to the palace in this weather?* It seemed impossible. She couldn't fly through the blizzard – if the magical ponies were having difficulties then there was no way she'd manage it. And she couldn't walk – the snow was much too thick on the ground for that.

But as she thanked the robin and let it back outside, Holly had an idea. What if she used her skis? She'd have to swap her diamond shoes for boots, but it would be worth it if she made it to the ball. She took off her shoes, pulled on her boots and grabbed her skis from the cupboard. Then she put on her warm turquoise winter coat over her wrap and dress. She pulled on her gloves, and thought about wearing her woollen hat too – but she really didn't want to mess up her hair!

Outside the cold wind blew so hard it hurt Holly's ears. She held up her umbrella as best she could, and pushed one foot forward in her skis. It hardly moved. She tried the other foot, hoping that she'd gradually get faster, but each time the ski got stuck in the snow. Holly tried lifting her feet up high like flippers, but she was getting nowhere. This was no good – at this rate it would be Boxing

Day before she got to the palace!

Trembling with disappointment, Holly turned round and went back inside her cottage. Sparkling snow dripped from her umbrella and skis. "Oh, I know I love the snow, but I wish it would stop just this once!" she said to herself as she slumped down on to her sofa. But the snow kept falling and whirling around, faster and faster. She'd never seen this much snow in fairyland before – not even at the top of Dream Mountain, which was covered in a blanket of snow in wintertime.

Holly took off her wrap. She should probably get changed – it was clear she'd never be able to get to the ball. She couldn't stop the tears that spilled from her eyes as she unzipped her dress. Her heart felt like a cold stone in her chest. She'd never been so disappointed.

Holly was about to slip out of her ball gown when she noticed something sparkling in the sky. It looked like a shining star. She put a hand to her mouth in thought. *It has to be worth a try, doesn't it? One last chance to get to the ball. . .* Holly had never wished upon a star before, and even though it felt a bit silly, she was desperate enough to try anything. She took a deep breath.

"Oh, little star, shining bright, help me get to the ball tonight. . ."

Chapter 6

Holly waited by the window, holding
her breath and hoping for some kind of
sign . . . but nothing came. She turned
away from the window sadly, and threw
some more fairy-dust on to the fire. Then
she heard a strange tinkling sound. Was
there something wrong with her clock?
No, it was still ticking away as usual. But
the tinkling noise was getting louder, and
it was coming from the window!

Holly zoomed over to it, her heart thumping. When she looked out, she couldn't believe her eyes. Standing outside her cottage was a beautiful silver sleigh, pulled by six shining white unicorns. She blinked in disbelief – one, two, three times. But it was still there!

Suddenly she saw that there was someone in the sleigh – someone with long white hair. Then she realized who it was and her heart nearly stopped completely. *The Snow Queen!* She was the very special fairy who delivered presents throughout fairyland on Christmas Eve. Holly had only heard about her in fairy tales – she'd never seen her before! The stunning fairy wore a thick white velvet cloak and had the largest wings Holly had ever seen, with shining silver tips. She had long, flowing ice-white hair and piercing light blue eyes.

Holly opened the window, wondering
what to say to the Snow Queen. She'd
never dreamt she'd meet her.

"Um . . . is everything OK, Snow
Queen?" she asked.

The fairy looked at Holly sadly and
shook her head. "Well, no, not really. You
see, I was in the middle of delivering
the Christmas presents to all the fairies
when the snowstorm turned really bad.
I'm afraid the unicorns have exhausted
themselves trying to fly through the
blizzard."

They did look tired, Holly realized. They were leaning their heads against each other, and their legs were trembling.

"But then I saw you looking up as we flew over Sparkle City. I know I don't usually allow fairies to see me, but this is an impossible situation, and I thought you might be able to help."

So that's *what the star was!* thought Holly.

"We desperately need more fairy-dust," the Snow Queen explained. "The dust will help us fly magically through the air, without the unicorns having to work so hard."

Holly gasped. It would be a disaster if the Snow Queen couldn't get the presents to everyone. All the fairies in fairyland would be so disappointed!

"Wait there!" said Holly, determined to help.

She closed the window, then ran into her bedroom, where her flying-piggy bank hovered from the ceiling on a thread of moth-silk. She pulled it down and emptied it out on to her bedside table. There wasn't as much fairy-dust inside as a few days ago, now that she'd bought so many things for the ball, but Holly had always liked saving. There had to be five handfuls at least! She grabbed two handfuls and ran outside, not thinking about the cold, and flung the magical dust over the unicorns and the sleigh.

Immediately the unicorns started to perk up, and the sleigh began to sparkle. The Snow Queen smiled. "Thank you, Holly, I'm sure that will help."

"I haven't finished yet — stay there!" Holly zoomed back inside her cottage, picked up two more handfuls of fairy-dust,

then carried them back outside and
threw them over the sleigh once again.

"Thank you from the bottom of my heart,"
said the queen as the sleigh began to rise
slowly into the air. "I believe that will work!"

Holly smiled and waved goodbye to the Snow Queen.

The beautiful white-haired fairy beamed. "Well, what are you waiting for? Jump in!"

"Really?" Holly asked in shock.

"Of course – if we hurry, you'll be just in time for the ball!"

"But how did you know I was invited?" Holly asked, surprised.

The Snow Queen gave her the tiniest wink, and Holly remembered that she was the most magical fairy of them all. Of course she knew Holly was going to the ball. She knew about *everything*.

"Just a second!" said Holly. She darted inside and put her dainty ball shoes and faux-fur wrap back on. As she flew outside again she pinched herself, unable to believe she was about to get a ride with the Snow Queen. But the special fairy was right before her eyes, beckoning Holly to sit beside her in the sleigh.

Holly fluttered up and sat down, and the sleigh rose higher and higher. As they floated upwards Holly watched her little cottage getting smaller, until it was just a tiny dot beneath them. Wow – she really was flying alongside the Snow Queen in a unicorn-pulled sleigh! The snow continued to fall around them, although Holly noticed that it was completely dry in the sleigh. How was that possible?

"Fairy magic," the Snow Queen said, as if she'd read Holly's mind.

Holly couldn't stop grinning. She held on tightly as the sleigh whizzed through the air, powered by the fairy-dust. She looked down at Sparkle City below, which looked like a blanket of white

sprinkled with Christmas lights.

"I'll drop you off at the ball," said the
Snow Queen, "and then continue with
my deliveries."

"Thank you so much," said Holly in a
small voice. "I really thought I'd never get
to the ball!" She looked at the unicorns.
Thankfully they seemed much happier

now they no longer had to work so hard to fly.

"Is there anything I can do in return for your help, Holly?" the Snow Queen asked.

Holly turned to the fairy in surprise. "But you've already given me a lift!" She couldn't think of anything else anyway – she was on the way to the most magical ball in all of fairyland.

"Oh, taking you to the ball is easy now we're powered by magic! Are you sure there's nothing else?"

Then it came to Holly – there *was* something she'd like to do. . .

"Well, actually, I have two very special friends who helped me get ready for the ball, even though they weren't invited. I'd like to do something to thank them, but I don't know what. . ."

The Snow Queen smiled and winked.
"Leave it with me," she replied.

Chapter 7

As they approached Glimmershine Palace,
Holly's mouth dropped open in amazement.
The grand building looked even more
beautiful than usual. Its turrets were
dotted with thousands of fairy lights, and
the grounds were covered by a carpet of
sparkling snow. To Holly's relief, it didn't look
like the palace had been badly affected by
the blizzard. Then she noticed that it wasn't
snowing at all here. Was this fairy magic too?

The Snow Queen pulled on the reins
of the sleigh and they whooshed down
towards the palace's cobbled driveway.
Holly couldn't think of a better way to
arrive at a ball!

"Thank you again, Snow Queen,"
said Holly solemnly as the sleigh landed
smoothly on a cushion of glistening snow.

The Snow Queen's eyes twinkled.

"It was my pleasure. I hope you have a magical evening!"

As soon as Holly had fluttered out of the sleigh, it rose back off the ground and sped into the night, turning into a shining dot in the sky once more. The journey had been so magical that now the Snow Queen had vanished, it almost felt like a dream. But Holly knew it was real, because she had made it to the ball against all the odds!

It wasn't until she walked through the grand arched doorway of the palace that Holly realized she hadn't even told the Snow Queen the names of her two best friends. How would she find them?

In the entrance hall, Holly gazed at the huge glass spiral staircase that wove up through the centre of the palace. It was hung with magnificent gold and

silver Christmas garlands and looked
so magical – almost as if Holly might
find an amazing adventure at the top.
She heard someone call her name and
looked around to see Princesses Buttercup,
Bluebell and Rosa, grinning and waving.

"Welcome to the Snowflake Ball!" said Rosa, beaming from ear to ear.

Bluebell gave Holly a hug. "We're so glad you managed to make it through the blizzard."

Holly smiled. "I nearly didn't!" She was about to tell the fairy princesses all about her lift with the Snow Queen – but then she changed her mind. She didn't know anyone else who'd seen the Snow Queen, and Holly was worried the princesses might not believe her. "But I'm here now! The palace looks stunning."

As the fairy princesses pointed out the Christmas decorations, Violet flew into the hall. "We've been working on them for months!" she said.

Two huge Christmas trees stood either side of the sweeping glass staircase, and these were lit up by hundreds of fairy lights and decorations.

"The baubles are made from gems that came all the way from Jewel Forest!" Rosa explained.

Holly fluttered closer to one of the fireplaces. Four very cute stockings made of glittery wool hung from the mantelpiece. "Ooh, where did these come from?" she asked. "I'd love to have one for my mantelpiece at home."

"I made them," said Buttercup in her soft, quiet voice. "I'm so glad you like them."

The fairy princesses led Holly into the banquet room, where the walls were covered in sparkling red-and-green bunting. At one end stood a Christmas tree even bigger than those she'd seen in the entrance hall. It was covered with so many sparkling baubles, gifts and ribbons that Holly could hardly see any green

beneath at all. The baubles floated above
the branches, glistening with fairy-dust,
making the tree look extra magical. At
the top was a silver star that spun slowly,
giving off showers of silver glitter as it
moved. At the other end of the room was
a mirrored dance floor in front of a stage.

Suddenly, a fairy-bunny tooted on a

trumpet. "That's to announce the start of dinner," explained Bluebell. She pointed to the circular dining tables that were dotted across the room. "All the seats have place names, so I hope you can find yours OK."

Holly nodded. "Thank you, Bluebell. I'm sure I'll be fine."

The room started to fill with beautifully dressed guests in all different types and colours of ball gowns. Holly said hello to a couple of fairies she knew, including Willa from Jewel Forest and Honey from Shimmer Island.

Holly fluttered among the tables, looking out for her name. It didn't take her too long to find the seat where the name "Holly" danced above the plate in sparkling fairy-dust – how magical!

Holly sat down on the cushioned red velvet chair and turned to say hello to her neighbour. To her delight, it was Princess Buttercup!

"Hello!" said Holly.

Buttercup grinned. "Hi, Holly! Oh, I can't wait for the banquet to begin – we've got lots of yummy food that we chose especially for the ball."

"Holly, is that you?" said a smooth voice behind her.

Holly turned to see who was sat the other side of her and squealed in delight – it was Snowdrop, from Dream Mountain! The two fairies were cousins and great friends – although they didn't see each other very often, as they lived so far apart. They had always found it funny that they both had wintry names. Snowdrop's waist-length hair had been piled up in a stunning bun on the top of her head, and she wore a gorgeous pink floor-length gown with sequins at the hem and on the sleeves.

"You look beautiful," said Holly.

"Thank you, Holly – and so do you!"

Moments later, the first course of the Snowflake Ball banquet was served by the fairy-helpers – tiny fairies with double wings who worked at the palace.

Holly stared at the food before her. It looked too good to eat! Star-shaped tomatoes were placed around the edge of the plate, and there were ribbons of beetroot piled in the centre with a scattering of pink walnuts on top. She pulled her Christmas cracker with Snowdrop, and they gasped as it shot out a burst of fairy-dust. This was followed by a tiara, which spun around and nestled on Holly's head, and a tiny present wrapped in golden paper. Holly opened it and let out a

squeak of happiness – it was a snowflake
ring that perfectly matched her dress!

Soon, everyone had pulled their magical
crackers and started to eat their food.
It tasted delicious! Fairy-helpers passed
around fresh warm bread rolls straight
from the oven, which Holly quickly
spread with glitter-butter from a little
bowl on the table.

The next course was a Christmas pie
filled with potatoes, turkey, parsnips and

smooth, creamy gravy. After she'd finished the last mouthful, Holly wasn't sure she could eat another thing — but then the fairy-helpers brought around snow cones, asking each guest which flavour they'd like.

"Oh, strawberry and lime, please!" said Holly. It was her favourite.

As the fairy-helpers cleared the tables, a band started up on the stage. Snowdrop nudged Holly. "The band is from Dream Mountain!" she told her. "The fairy princesses asked them to come along especially."

Holly looked over and gasped — the band was a group of dragonflies, which darted in and out of little silver harps to make the music.

Soon Holly was on the dance floor, along with the rest of the guests. They twirled and spun around, dancing to "Christmas Tree Flutter", "Fairy Special Christmas" and lots of other Christmas songs. Time passed so quickly that Holly couldn't believe it when the fairy-bunny

blew on the trumpet once more. Was it time to go home already?

As everyone turned to look at
the bunny, she squeaked, "It is now
midnight – officially Christmas Day!
Please could I ask everyone to go outside?"

The fairies began filing out of the rear
banquet-room door. *Whatever can it be?*
wondered Holly.

Chapter 8

Holly was very glad of her faux-fur wrap as the fairies stood shivering in the palace gardens, waiting to find out what was going on. Suddenly, out of nowhere, the most amazing shower of shooting stars began to fly out over Lily-pad Lake. Red stars, green stars, yellow stars and purple stars – Holly had never seen anything like it before!

Princess Rosa came up beside Holly.

"We have mermaid guests from Glitter Ocean too – they're having a party in the lake, so they can see the shooting star display just as well as we can!"

That's a lovely idea, thought Holly, glad

* * * 75 * * *

that the mermaids weren't missing out.

The shooting stars kept coming, and were now spinning in circles like Catherine wheels. Everyone oohed and aahed and clapped as the stars kept shooting above them, but Holly's eye was suddenly drawn by something else, just off to the right of the stars. If she wasn't mistaken, it looked like a tiny sleigh pulled by unicorns. Had the Snow Queen returned? A shiver of excitement ran down her spine.

The display ended with a burst of silver stars that rushed up into the air, darted about and, to Holly's delight, spelled out the words "Merry Christmas"!

Everyone whooped and cheered, then hugged each other.

"That was incredible!" Holly said to Rosa as she gave her a huge hug. "Thank you so much!"

The guests began to make their way back inside the palace, chattering about the shooting stars and how wonderful they were. Just when Holly didn't think the ball could get any better, she spotted an enormous pile of presents that had appeared under the Christmas tree in the banquet hall.

All the fairy guests stood around the tree in awe. "The Snow Queen has been!" said Bluebell, dancing from foot to foot.

The fairy princesses started handing out the presents to their guests. When Holly opened her parcel, she shrieked in delight – there, nestled in silver tissue paper, was a beautiful woollen stocking, just like the ones Buttercup had made! She showed her present to Snowdrop, who had unwrapped a gorgeous pink scarf, threaded with moth-silk.

"I can't wait until next year to use it."
Holly stroked the soft knitted stocking.
"Actually, I'm going to put it up on
my mantelpiece right away – then I can
admire it all year round!"

As she was talking, Holly noticed
movement from behind the last few
presents still underneath the Christmas
tree. She squinted at them and moved
closer.

"SURPRISE!" Summer and May
jumped out from the presents, waving

tinsel. "Merry Christmas!"

"Oh my fairyness!" cried Holly, her heart almost thumping right out of her chest with excitement. "I can't believe it! Were you invited to the ball all along? It's so lovely to have you here!" Just when she'd thought all of her wishes had come true, this was the best surprise of them all!

Summer, who was dressed in a beautiful royal blue satin gown, beamed. "No, we weren't invited — well, not at first, anyway. . ."

May, who wore a gorgeous turquoise maxi-dress, leant close to Holly's ear. "We were at my house having dinner when the Snow Queen appeared," she explained in a whisper. "We couldn't believe it. She told us she'd arranged a last-minute invitation!"

"She brought us here in her sleigh,"

added Summer. "It was such a magical ride!"

Holly grinned. She knew just how magical it was. *But not quite as magical as this very moment*, she thought as she hugged her two best friends and wished them a very Happy Christmas. The Snow Queen had thought of the most perfect way to thank Holly – inviting Summer and May!

The band began to play once more and everyone fluttered back on to the dance floor. The ball was far from over. The three friends danced and twirled each other about, singing along to the Christmas songs and laughing. Now all of Holly's wishes had really come true. She'd never forget such a wonderful Christmas, especially now she got to share it with the best and kindest friends in all of fairyland!

If you enjoyed this

Fashion Fairy Princess

book then why not visit our
magical new website!

- ✿ Explore the enchanted world of
  the fashion fairy princesses
- ✿ Find out which fairy princess
  you are
- ✿ Download sparkly screensavers
- ✿ Make your own tiara
- ✿ Colour in your own picture frame
  and much more!

fashionfairyprincess.com

Turn the page for a sneak peek of another
Fashion Fairy Princess adventure...

Chapter 1

"Please could you pass me the petal pancakes, Buttercup?" asked Violet, eyeing the tall stack of fluffy pink cakes hungrily. "They look delicious."

"They are," said Bluebell, pouring rose-coloured syrup on to her second helping. "I think they might be the nicest I've ever tasted."

Buttercup passed the silver plate of

pancakes to her friend. It was a sunny Saturday morning and the fashion fairy princesses – Violet, Rosa, Buttercup and Bluebell – were having breakfast on the jewelled patio of Glimmershine Palace. All around them the glittering pink and purple flowers of the palace's gardens fluttered in the gentle breeze.

"It's such a beautiful day," said Buttercup, taking a sip of nectar from the flower-shaped glass in front of her. "I can't wait to get down to the palace stables."

"Oh look," said Violet, "here's Ferdinand with the fairy-mail. I wonder if he has anything exciting for me."

Ferdinand was a beautiful metallic blue firefly and a fairy-flyer. The fairy-flyers picked up and delivered the fashion fairy princesses' fairy-mail from all over Sparkle City.

Violet looked a little disappointed as Ferdinand buzzed quickly past her chair. He also passed Rosa and Bluebell but landed gently next to a surprised Buttercup.

"I wasn't expecting anything," said Buttercup excitedly as she thanked Ferdinand and reached into his saddlebag. When she pulled out her hand, she was holding a large gold glittering shell.

"What a beautiful shell," said Bluebell.

"It looks like it came from Glitter Ocean," said Rosa, peering closer. "Do you know someone from Glitter Ocean, Buttercup?"

"Only my Great-aunt Melinda. She's a mermaid and lives near Coral Castle with the other merpeople," answered Buttercup, examining the shell carefully, "but I haven't heard from her since last year's

Annual Fairy Festival."

"Aren't you going to open it?" said Violet, desperate to know what was inside. "Perhaps it's a present."

Buttercup looked at the large, flat shell in her hand and tried to open it with her delicate fingers, but nothing happened.

"Let me have a go," said Violet, reaching for the shell.

"Violet, it's Buttercup's invitation. Let her open it," said Rosa gently. "Buttercup, why don't you try using a little fairy-dust? Perhaps it was closed with fairy magic."

"Good idea, Rosa," said Violet. "Sorry, Buttercup, I was only trying to help."

Buttercup took out a small pouch of fairy-dust from the skirt of her dress and sprinkled a little over the shell. With a puff of golden glitter, the shell opened to reveal a shining yellow invitation. . .

Get creative with the fashion fairy princesses in this magical sticker-activity book!

With over **500** stickers

Fashion Fairy Princess

Christmas Wishes
STICKER BOOK

Full of stickering, doodling, puzzling fun!